Santa's Ark

First published in the United States and Canada by
The Millbrook Press, Inc.
2 Old New Milford Road,
Brookfield, CT 06804

Devised and produced by
Tucker Slingsby Ltd,
Berkeley House,
73 Upper Richmond Road,
London SW15 2SZ

Copyright © 1997 Tucker Slingsby Ltd
Copyright illustrations © 1997 Cliff Wright

With thanks to Sue Seddon

Library of Congress Cataloging-in-Publication Data

Wright, Cliff.
Santa's ark / by Cliff Wright.
      p.   cm.
Summary: A naughty little reindeer that wants to see the
world stows away aboard Santa's sleigh and invites other
baby animals to join him at each stop Santa makes.
  ISBN 0-7613-0299-9 (trade) ISBN 0-7613-0314-6 (lib. bdg.)
  [1. Reindeer—Fiction. 2. Animals—Fiction.
  3. Santa Claus—Fiction. 4. Christmas—Fiction.]   I. Title.
PZ7.W9347San   1997
[E]—dc21   97-11228
                                                   CIP
                                                    AC

Printed in Singapore through Printlink International
Color reproduction by Bright Arts Graphics, Singapore

Santa's Ark

by Cliff Wright

The Millbrook Press, Inc.
Brookfield, Connecticut

It was Christmas Eve. The bright lights of Santa's workshop shone across the snowy North Pole. Santa gathered the reindeer together and harnessed each one to his sleigh.

"Only the presents to load, and we're on our way!" shouted Santa.

"Nearly ready," said Santa as he loaded the last and the biggest present onto the sleigh.

It was Santa's busiest night of the year. He was so busy that he didn't notice the little reindeer peeping through the window; so busy that he didn't see the little reindeer sneak through the door of his workshop.

Santa was so busy that he didn't notice the little reindeer creep onto the sleigh and hide under the presents. The stowaway was just in time. Santa's reindeer were already stamping their feet. Very soon they would be flying through the sky.

"Christmas crackers!" exclaimed Santa. "Off we go." And the reindeer raced across the snow until the sleigh rose into the twinkling sky.

As they soared among the frost-bright stars the little reindeer peeped out. A long, long way below, the snow sparkled with glittering lights.

To the little reindeer, the world looked like a great big Christmas cake. All the mountains and houses looked like toys. And Santa still didn't see his excited little passenger.

Whoosh! The sleigh swooped down and landed in the snow. As Santa went to deliver his first sack-load of presents the little reindeer poked his head up and then slipped out of the sleigh.

"Hello. Who are you?" asked a baby polar bear.

"I'm a reindeer and I'm off to see the world," he told the curious bear. "You can come too, but be quick, before Santa sees."

So the baby polar bear climbed aboard and the sleigh took off again. A seal watched the sleigh disappear into the night sky, and he wondered where it was going. For a minute, he wished he'd gone too.

They flew on. The sharp air roared in the little reindeer's ears and froze his nose—although the polar bear seemed to enjoy the frosty ride. The sleigh landed again, and Santa disappeared down a chimney.

A cat and a dog ran out of the house to see what was going on.

"Hello," said the little reindeer. "We're off to see the world. Why don't you come too? Quick, before Santa sees."

At first the cat and the dog were a little shy. The sleigh looked very exciting, but they weren't quite sure.

"We'll have great fun," said the little reindeer.

So the cat and dog jumped on board and the sleigh took off.

In Africa they landed with a bump. When the animals peeped out, they saw a baby elephant.

"Hello," said the little reindeer. "That's a big nose. What's it for?"

"This!" said the elephant and squirted them with water.

"Lovely!" they spluttered. "Come and see the world with us. Quick, before Santa sees." And together they heaved the elephant on board.

"Just one more push and you'll be in the sleigh," puffed the baby polar bear.

"Christmas crackers!" said Santa as they flew on. "This sleigh seems to be getting heavier and heavier."

Skimming over mountain tops, the sleigh stopped in China. There they saw a baby panda eating bamboo.

"We're off to see the world," they cried. "You can come too. Quick, before Santa sees."

So the panda clambered aboard Santa's sleigh and snuggled down.

The sleigh flew on to
Australia and landed on a beach.

"Wow!" said the naughty little
reindeer. "Look at those big
waves. Let's surf!"

While Santa searched for
chimneys and his team of
reindeer snoozed, the little
animals went surfing on the
big blue waves.

On the beach they met a baby
kangaroo.

"Hop on board and see the
world with us. Quick, before Santa
sees," said the little reindeer.

They flew **on** to the South Pole and landed near a
penguin who was ice-sliding.

"Hello," said the penguin, "come and join in." So the little
friends started sliding down the hill too. They were soon as
warm as toast and having a great time.

"Come around the world
with us," said the little reindeer.
"Quick, before Santa sees."
The penguin stopped sliding,
and climbed into the sleigh.

The sleigh left the snowy wastes and flew above wild,
green jungles. In a hot, steamy rainforest in South America,
they saw a little monkey swinging from the trees by its tail.

"Hello," said the little reindeer, wishing he had a clever
tail like that. "We're traveling around the world.
Come with us. Quick, before Santa sees!"
So the monkey swung on board.

By now, the sleigh was very crowded.

"Christmas crackers!" exclaimed Santa as they flew on to
North America. "I've delivered nearly all the presents,
but my sleigh seems to be heavier than ever."

Miles high above New York, the little reindeer
scrambled to get a good look at the Empire State Building.
But he leaned too far and tumbled out of the sleigh. The
polar bear, the dog and the cat, the panda, the kangaroo, the
penguin, and the monkey fell after him. Only the little
elephant clung onto the sleigh.

"Hang on, hang on!" she cried, and all the animals hung on
with claws, paws, beaks, and tails. Then the elephant heaved
and heaved and heaved again until she had pulled them all
back into the sleigh. And still Santa did not see them.

"All presents delivered," said Santa. "Time to go home,"
and he steered the big reindeer high over the ocean.
But they were very tired.
  "What's wrong, my friends?" Santa asked his reindeer.
  "It's the sleigh, Santa," they replied. "It's too heavy."

Santa turned around and nearly jumped out
of his skin. The sleigh was full of animals!
  "Jumping jingle bells!" shouted Santa.
  "It's not Santa's sleigh, it's Santa's ark!"
  They flew so slowly across the sky that
the sleigh went into a nose dive.

KER-SPLASH! went the sleigh as it hit the sea.
"Christmas crackers!" said Santa.
"That's done it. Mrs. Santa will be madder
than a melting snowman if we're not
home for breakfast."

Suddenly the sleigh was being lifted up and out of the sea.

"I'll take you home," boomed a voice nearby.

A baby whale had come to their rescue and all the stowaways climbed onto his back. The baby whale's mother swam alongside to keep them company.

The baby whale was so big that there was room on his back
for all the animals, Santa, and the sleigh too. There was much
excitement as they headed for the North Pole—and breakfast....

The dog and kangaroo danced while the panda gazed in
wonder at the snowy mountains. Penguin was so excited he dived into the
sea and swam on in front. Even the little reindeer was glad to be home.

Soon they were back
at Santa's house. They were all very
hungry and Mrs. Santa gave them a
most magnificent breakfast. The little
reindeer's mother peeped in at the
window, happy to see her little
stowaway safe and sound.

After a visit to Santa's workshop,
the little friends were taken home to
their families.

"You're a naughty little reindeer," said
his mother when the others had left.
 "Sorry," said the tired young reindeer.
 "One day you'll be big enough to pull
Santa's sleigh yourself, so don't sneak
on board again," his mother told him.

It was Christmas morning
and the little reindeer knew Santa had
lots of presents waiting for him.
He was so excited. He couldn't wait to
open them, but he felt very sleepy....
Merry Christmas, little reindeer!

JANE YOLEN

KING
Long Shanks

ILLUSTRATED BY
Victoria Chess

HARCOURT BRACE & COMPANY

San Diego   New York   London

This story is based on Hans Christian Andersen's
"The Emperor's New Clothes," one of the more than 150 wonderful
stories to flow from the nineteenth-century Danish storyteller's pen.
Of course, Andersen's emperor and court and the tailors were
humans, not frogs. But I thought it might be fun
to view them webbed and green.
—J. Y.

Library of Congress Cataloging-in-Publication Data
Yolen, Jane.
King Long Shanks/written by Jane Yolen; illustrated by Victoria Chess—1st ed.
p.   cm.
Retelling of: The emperor's new clothes.
Summary: Although he hates their poor poetry, a frog king agrees to let two flattering scoundrels
create an outfit for him that will show off his fine, long, strong legs and test the loyalty of his subjects.
ISBN 0-15-200013-5
[1. Fairy tales. 2. Frogs—Fiction.] I. Chess, Victoria, ill.
II. Andersen, H. C. (Hans Christian), 1805–1875. Kejserens nye klæder. English. III. Title.
PZ8.Y78Ki   1998
[Fic]—dc20   94-48359

C E G F D B

Printed in Singapore

The illustrations in this book were done in
Winsor & Newton liquid watercolors, Schmeincke regular watercolors,
Prisma pencils, and Rotring technical inks and pens on
Langton watercolor paper by Daler & Rowney.
The display type was set in Fontesque.
The text type was set in Adroit.
Color separations by United Graphic Pte. Ltd., Singapore
Printed and bound by Tien Wah Press, Singapore
This book was printed on totally chlorine-free Nymolla Matte Art paper.
Production supervision by Stanley Redfern
Designed by Linda Lockowitz

For all the students
who refuse to dissect frogs
in biology class
—J. Y.

To Arietta,
Daniel, and Sam
—V. C.

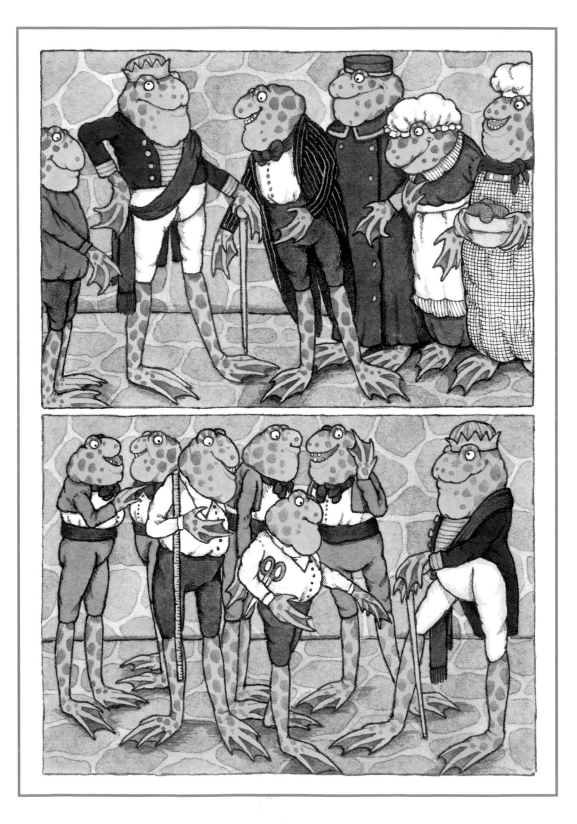

KING LONG SHANKS had very good legs and was a nice shade of green. Everyone said so. So it had to be true.

The cook said it.

The gardener said it.

The butler, maid, and doorman said it.

The lords-in-waiting said it.

And the two visiting tailors said it, too. Not once but many times.

"Fine legs," said the small tailor.

"Fine long legs," said the tall tailor.

"Fine long strong legs," they said together. "And a very nice shade of green."

So when the two tailors added, "We have just the thing to show off those fine long strong legs, Your Majesty," King Long Shanks ordered: "Tell me."

So they did. The small tailor stretched very high (to make himself taller). And the tall tailor squatted very low (to make himself smaller). Then they whispered simultaneously and at the same time in King Long Shanks' ears.

> The cloth is green,
> The cloth is blue,
> The very shade
> That's right for you.
>
> The cloth is blue,
> The cloth is red,
> To match the jewel
> Inside your head.
>
> The cloth is red,
> The cloth is gold,
> And only the true
> and good
> and honest
> and smart
> and loyal
> Can it behold.

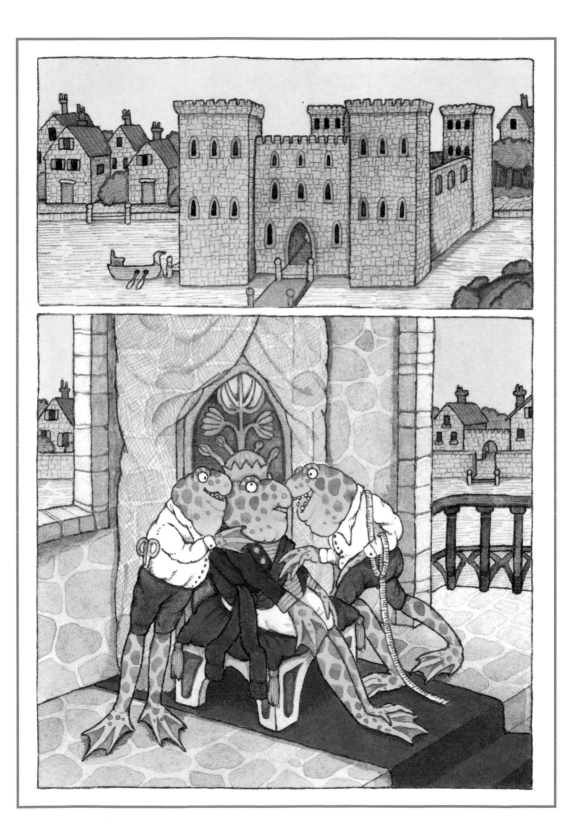

"What do you mean?" roared King Long Shanks. He was not fond of poetry, especially poetry that bumped in the wrong places and pretended to mean much more than it did. It made him go all cranky. "How can there be a cloth that is green and blue and red and gold? How can it match my head and the jewel inside it? How did you know about that jewel, anyway? It's a family secret."

He had many questions.

The tailors had many answers.

"It's a plaid cloth, sire," they said.

"It's a magic plaid cloth, sire," they said.

"It's a mysterious magic plaid cloth, sire," they said.

"And besides," they said, "it's very expensive."

Now, King Long Shanks did not know a lot about fashion, but he *did* know that expense was a good part of it.

"Show me," he ordered.

So the two tailors held their hands out, first wide apart, then close together. "What do you think?" they asked.

Since there appeared to be nothing between their hands but air, King Long Shanks did not know *what* to think. So he did what he always did when he wanted to pretend he understood something and didn't. He looked at the ceiling, hummed his favorite pond tune, and waited for a passing fly.

KA-ZAAAACK! He caught the fly with his tongue, then looked back at the tailors with a seriously informed expression.

"It's an *invisible* plaid cloth," said the tall tailor.

"Only someone who is true, good, honest, and smart can see the cloth," added the small tailor.

"And loyal," reminded the tall tailor.

"No one can question *my* loyalty," said King Long Shanks, "since it is loyalty to me."

"No one does," the tailors said quickly. "But the cloth is a sure way to check on the rest of the kingdom."

King Long Shanks swallowed the fly. "Then I will want a complete outfit," he said. He touched the air between the tailors, as if feeling a piece of cloth. "Lovely color." Then he turned on his fine long strong legs and leaped away.

THE TAILORS SPENT MANY HOURS sewing their invisible cloth. The small tailor sewed large stitches. The tall tailor sewed tiny stitches. They cut and shaped and measured and cut again.

"Mother," said the princess one day as she watched them work, "there is nothing there. No cloth, no coat, no . . ."

"Hush," said the queen, "or your father will think you disloyal. Eat your flies."

"Mother," said the prince, "there really *is* nothing there. No pants, no socks, no . . ."

"Double hush," said the queen. "Loyalty begins at home. Your bugs are getting cold."

And because the queen and the princess and the prince said nothing, no one else said anything at all. Not the cook. Not the gardener. Not the butler, maid, or doorman. Not the lords-in-waiting.

And certainly not the tailors, who were, after all, being paid for their work.

Since no one said anything, King Long Shanks believed what he wanted to believe. Or needed to believe. Or thought he believed. Except for once, when he asked, "Are you *sure* that cloth is . . . well . . . right for me?"

The small tailor stretched himself very high (to make himself taller). And the tall tailor squatted very low (to make himself smaller). Then they whispered simultaneously and at the same time in King Long Shanks' ears.

The cloth is short,
The cloth is long,
For you it's right,
Another—wrong.

The cloth is narrow,
The cloth is wide,
So you can wear
Your clothes with pride.

The cloth is thick,
The cloth is thin,
And only the true
                and good
                and honest
                and smart
                and loyal—

"I know, I know," interrupted King Long Shanks because he hated their poetry, and besides he didn't want them to suspect he couldn't see anything. KA-ZAAAACK! He ate another fly hastily and felt exceedingly cranky.

"You know everything, sire," said the small tailor.

"That's why you get the big bucks, Your Majesty," said the tall tailor.

And then they smiled simultaneously and at the same time. It was not a pretty sight.

AND SO THE TAILORS continued to sew on an invisible cloth that no one dared say was not there for fear of being thought a ninny, a nonny, a numbskull, or a nincompoop. And disloyal besides.

Days went by. Weeks even. And at last it was time for the Summer Parade, when lily pads opened their big broad petals and the air fair hummed with insects.

King Long Shanks called the tailors to his throne room. "Will my new outfit be ready for the big parade?" he asked.

"That is exactly what we have been aiming for, sire," said the small tailor.

"We will sew you into it ourselves," the tall tailor added.

"For all your loyal subjects to see," they said together.

And on the morning of the parade, the two tailors, their hands full of the invisible cloth, dressed the king themselves.

First they put on his invisible shirt.

Then his invisible shorts.

Then his invisible jacket and cloak and socks and shoes.

"We have a hat as well, Your Majesty," they said.

"I will wear my crown," King Long Shanks said. "So my loyal subjects will know me."

They brought him the royal mirror.

King Long Shanks stared and stared.

"Toadally majestic," said the tall tailor.

"Ribeting," said the small tailor.

And they laughed secretly behind their hands simultaneously and at the same time.

King Long Shanks did not notice them laugh. He was too busy staring.

"The mirror cannot, of course, show you how wonderful the outfit is," said the small tailor.

"After all," added the tall tailor, "a mirror is not true or good or honest or smart."

"Or loyal," they said together.

"Well, at least you are right about one thing," said King Long Shanks, glancing at his reflection one last time.

"We are?" they asked.

"This outfit certainly shows off my fine long strong legs." He turned, went down the hall, and out into the courtyard, where the Summer Parade was about to begin.

The queen and prince and princess were waiting there, dressed in their finery. The cook and the gardener were there as well. And so were the butler, maid, and doorman, and all the lords-in-waiting. And round them were the guards from the guardhouse, the soldiers from the armory, the townsfolk and farmfolk and the folk who tended the woods. In fact, everyone from the entire kingdom was there, waiting to walk in the parade that wound down from the palace to the pond, where the king would declare the opening of Summer.

Only the two tailors were missing. They had already collected their pay and were well on their way to the next kingdom.

There was a murmur when King Long Shanks appeared, dressed in his invisible clothes. But the queen had warned them all. And since they were all really terribly loyal to their king, the parade started with not one comment.

The parade was halfway to the pond when a little tad spoke up. "Mama," she said. "Papa—look at the king. He has no . . ."

"Hush!" her mama and papa said.

They were three-fourths of the way to the pond when the tad spoke up again. "But Mama, but Papa, really, King Long Shanks has no . . ."

"Hush!" said her mama and papa and her brothers and sisters and cousins. "Hush! We are loyal to our king."

They were all the way down to the pond when the tad spoke again, in a voice the waters carried. "Mama, Papa, brothers and sisters and cousins— King Long Shanks is bare! His fine long strong legs and—*everything*!"

Just then a breeze rippled the pond and it looked like all the lily pads were laughing. That set the child and her brothers and sisters and cousins and mama and papa—and finally the woodfolk and farmfolk and townsfolk to grinning. And *that* set the soldiers from the armory, the guards from the guardhouse, the butler and maid and doorman to giggling. And *that* set the cook and gardener to guffawing. And *that* made the prince and princess collapse in the green grass in hysterics.

Only the queen was somber. Silently she tore off a piece of her own beautiful gown and covered King Long Shanks with it, for she was the most loyal one of them all.

As to the tailors, they never entered *that* particular kingdom again with their magic cloth. But they played their same trick on one hundred and one other kings and emperors around the world. You may have heard of them.

However, none of those one hundred and one other kings and emperors had legs nearly as good or fine or long or strong—or green—as King Long Shanks. Of that I am sure.

▲▲▲

MORAL

True loyalty cannot be measured as simply as cloth.
But it covers a lot more than legs.

▼▼▼